Because of you, Victor's Dream will be gifted to a child!

THIS BOOK IS PRESENTED TO

....

By

....

Date

....

For

....

DEDICATED TO

Bera Y. Owens
devoted, beloved teacher and librarian
advocate for literacy
example of living Christianity
famous for
chocolate pies, fudge, figs, and
Sunday dinners that always
had room at the table for
any and all children

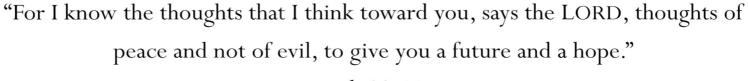

"For I know the thoughts that I think toward you, says the LORD, thoughts of peace and not of evil, to give you a future and a hope."

Jeremiah 29:11 *NKJV*

VICTOR'S DREAM

by

DEBORAH EHLER POLSTON

dawson media®

SCREEEEEECH . . . whoooooshhh! Brakes squealed and thumped loudly as the bus rolled to a stop outside the main entrance of Safe Haven Children's Home. Victor James grabbed his book bag and slung it onto his back. With his shoulders slumped and eyes glued to the floor, Victor made his way down the aisle hoping no one would notice him. But it didn't matter . . . .

"It's 'home sweet home' for you, Orphan Boy!" Jake mocked loudly as Victor stepped off the bus. The other boys laughed with approval.

It was always the same. Sometimes Victor wished he could just fly away to live in a normal neighborhood with a regular family like everyone else. But after seven years of being bounced from one foster home to another, and eight years at Safe Haven, Victor knew this was the closest thing to a home he would ever have. Besides, his younger brother Chase and baby sister Gracie lived here too. He couldn't leave them, especially since he was the real reason they still hadn't been adopted. The State always tried to keep brothers and sisters together—but who would want a fifteen-year-old kid with two younger siblings?

Victor walked slowly past Anderson House, which was home to the younger children. Next was the blue and white Toole House for boys and then the green Forester House for girls. Finally, Victor reached the oldest house on campus, a large brick colonial with a wide, welcoming front porch. Connor House sheltered three sibling groups, including Victor, Chase, and Gracie, who were cared for by Don and Emily Connor.

"I'm home, Ms. Emily!" Victor called as he walked through the front door.

"Victor, I'm in the laundry room. Your snack is on the kitchen table," Mrs. Connor's voice echoed down the hall. "How was your day?"

"It was okay," Victor answered.

"Well, finish your homework before the kids get home."

"I got it done at school!" Victor went through the kitchen and grabbed the red apple and cookie Mrs. Connor had left for him. As he passed by his room, Victor tossed his book bag on the bed and was already out the back door before he heard Mrs. Connor calling after him.

"Be back in an hour to help the kids with their homework!"

"Okay!"

Behind Connor House was a big open field where all of the little kids liked to play ball. At the edge of the field was a huge oak tree that was Victor's favorite hideout.

When he reached the tree, Victor stepped up on an old rusty wheelbarrow and reached as high as he could, grabbing hold of the lowest branch. Victor pulled himself up, climbed nearly to the top, and settled comfortably into a seat that seemed to be made just for him by three intersecting branches. He leaned back and rested his head against the knobby bark, breathing in the strong aroma of freshly cut grass. Feeling relaxed for the first time all day, Victor closed his eyes and listened to the gentle rustle of leaves above his head and the cheerful sound of busy birds on a beautiful spring day.

Suddenly, Victor heard a commotion at the base of the tree.

"Throw him in this pit and leave him! We can take his new coat that Father gave him and make it look like an animal attacked him."

Victor leaned over and called down through the branches. "What's going on?"

Whoever was down there ignored him. "Look! Here comes a band of traders. Maybe we can sell him! They'll never believe he's our brother. We won't have to kill him, and we'll be rid of this foolish dreamer once and for all!"

Victor watched in disbelief as the traders pulled a boy about his own age out of a deep hole and handed several coins to a mean-looking man holding a colorful coat. As the man left with his brothers, Victor leaned down a little farther to see what would happen next.

Ahhhhhh! Victor cried out as he lost his balance and fell to the ground with a loud thump. Embarrassed, he looked around at the sandy desert terrain and tugged on his strange tunic and woven sandals. *Where am I? What happened to the grass? Where are my clothes?* He wondered.

The startled traders recovered quickly. "Spying were you? Get up, boy! We'll take you with us, two slaves for the price of one," said the leader. "Tie them together and get moving! It's a long journey to Egypt!"

Victor turned to the boy next to him. "Uh, I'm not . . . where . . . where am I?"

"My name is Joseph, I am Jacob's son. Who do you belong to?"

"Belong to? I don't really know. I don't belong to anyone. This doesn't make any sense. I must be dreaming!"

"Dreaming is what got me here too. Nice to meet you . . . what did you say your name was?" Joseph asked.

"My name is Victor."

"You will be Victor, son of Jacob. You do belong!"

"Are you really Joseph? I think I've heard about you and your family before."

"I can't say I've heard of you, but I guess we'll have plenty of time to get to know each other now." Joseph said with a serious tone.

"Quiet! No more talking, slaves!" The leader jabbed his walking stick into Victor's back and shoved him ahead.

With wide, frightened eyes, Victor glanced over at Joseph and was confused by how calm he looked. Didn't he know that they were in big trouble?

Time seemed to fly by and before Victor knew it they had arrived in Egypt. The traders quickly sold Joseph and Victor as slaves to a man named Potiphar, who decided that Joseph was to serve at the main house, while Victor would be taken to work in the stable where the animals were kept.

As Victor was led away, he looked back at Joseph, his only friend in this strange place. Victor was scared, but Joseph nodded and smiled as if to say that everything would be fine.

When Victor reached the stable, he was told to get some rest, for work would start early the next day. Victor found a quiet corner and spread out some hay to make a bed. Lying down, he looked up at the heavy support beams overhead and thought he had never felt so tired before in his life. Falling asleep would be easy.

Victor jolted awake to the wild sounds of miniature cow-boys and Indians. Not knowing where he was, he twisted around and lost his balance. As he toppled over, Victor tried to grab hold of something to break his fall. But he bumped and crashed through the leaves and branches . . . down, down, down . . . finally landing seat-first in the rusty old wheelbarrow on the ground.

Stunned and disoriented, Victor looked around and saw the familiar green field now swarming with the younger children who were home from school. Several of them were making a beeline straight for him.

"Victor! Are you okay?"

Once Victor grunted that he was fine, the children laughed hysterically.

"Thanks, guys, I love you too." he said sarcastically under his breath.

That evening at Connor House, everyone gathered in the kitchen before dinner. Mrs. Connor gave Victor a funny look when she saw the scrapes on his arms and legs. "Did something happen to you today, Victor?" she asked.

Victor looked embarrassed. "I lost my balance and fell out of the tree."

He was relieved when Mr. Connor came into the kitchen and interrupted the discussion. Soon everyone sat down to eat.

"Well, how was your day, kids?" Mr. Connor asked, looking around the table expectantly. "Did you learn anything or meet someone new?"

Victor spoke up. "Well, I met someone new . . . in a way. I had a pretty cool dream."

"Really? What happened?" Mr. Connor asked.

"I met Joseph from the Bible and traveled with him to Egypt."

The younger kids giggled.

"Go ahead and laugh, but it was like I was really there. I was watching when Joseph's brothers sold him as a slave to a bunch of traders and left him behind. That's when I fell out of the tree and they tied me up with Joseph and took us to Egypt to be sold as slaves."

"That's quite a dream, Victor. Sounds like God allowed you walk with Joseph for a while so you could learn something from him," Mr. Connor said.

"It was amazing. I never heard Joseph complain, not once! His brothers did a really bad thing to him, but he stayed calm. I don't think I could have done that, I would have fought back."

"You talk about him like he's real or something," said Chase. "You sound kind of crazy."

"Thanks, Chase," Victor answered dryly.

"Chase, sometimes God gives us dreams that seem very real, usually when He wants to teach us something important," Mrs. Connor explained.

"Victor, why do you think Joseph was so calm and peaceful?" Mr. Connor asked.

"He knew God would take care of him, I guess."

"That's right!" he answered. "Victor, you can have that same peace too. God promises to take care of all of us. If He feeds the birds, how much more do you think He cares for you? He made you in His very own image."

"You say that to us all the time!" said Gracie in her sweet little voice.

"Well, that's because it's true!" answered Mr. Connor with a grin.

That night, just before bedtime, Mr. Connor stopped by Victor's room.

"I'm glad you shared your dream with us tonight, Victor. God is raising you up to be a leader."

"Me, a leader?"

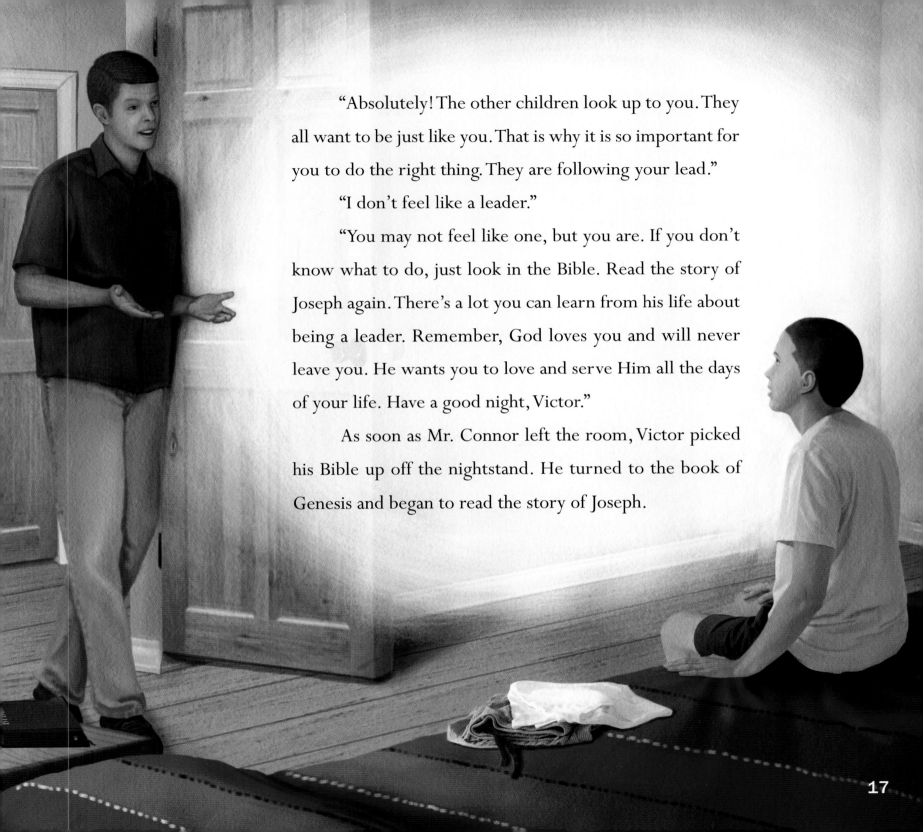

"Absolutely! The other children look up to you. They all want to be just like you. That is why it is so important for you to do the right thing. They are following your lead."

"I don't feel like a leader."

"You may not feel like one, but you are. If you don't know what to do, just look in the Bible. Read the story of Joseph again. There's a lot you can learn from his life about being a leader. Remember, God loves you and will never leave you. He wants you to love and serve Him all the days of your life. Have a good night, Victor."

As soon as Mr. Connor left the room, Victor picked his Bible up off the nightstand. He turned to the book of Genesis and began to read the story of Joseph.

The early morning sun was peeking through the rafters when Victor opened his eyes. He could smell the scent of hay and the pungent odor of sweaty animals. The wooden beams over his head looked vaguely familiar.

Whoa! Suddenly Victor was wide awake. *Animals? Where in the world am I?!*

The same moment Victor realized that he was back in Potiphar's barn, he heard someone barking orders at him from outside.

"Get out here, boy! Fill the buckets with feed and load them onto the cart. The palace animals need to be fed right away. You'd better quit your daydreaming and get a move on if you don't want a flogging!"

Hurrying as fast as he could, Victor filled the heavy containers and loaded them onto the pull cart. Somehow, he managed to get the donkey harnessed and began leading the plodding animal uphill toward the palace.

In the distance, Victor could see Joseph walking toward him.

"Victor, son of Jacob, where have you been?" Joseph asked with surprise.

Victor noticed that Joseph looked different. His clothes were neat, clean, and rich looking. And he seemed older and important, as though he were in charge.

"Well . . . I'm not sure how I got here, but a big man at the stable told me to haul feed up to the palace," Victor answered.

Joseph laughed. "Don't worry about that now, friend. I can have someone else tend to your chores for a while. Why don't you come have lunch with me at Potiphar's table? We have some catching up to do. Many things have changed since I saw you last."

At lunch Victor looked around the palace with awe. "Joseph, how did you get all this stuff? You were sold as a slave just like me and now you have cool clothes, your own chariot and horses, and people listen to you."

"God has given me favor, Victor, so I can fulfill His purpose. All of God's children can walk in that same favor to carry out what God wants them to do. You do belong to God, don't you, Victor?"

"Sure I do, but look at me, I'm not anything special. You have so much more than I do. Does that mean God loves you more?"

"Not at all, Victor, you are very special to God. It doesn't matter where God puts you, only how you handle it. Just like you, I tended the animals.

I was a shepherd, not a very impressive job. But I did it with all my might and ability and praised God everyday for loving me and watching over me."

"Back home I'm a pretty good student and make good grades," Victor said. "My house parents put me in charge of helping the younger children with their homework every day."

"See what I mean?" Joseph said. "Because you were faithful with your studies and helping the children, God is now putting you in charge of something greater. Just like your name, you are a 'victor,' not a victim. You were made to overcome every obstacle with God's help. So look up, my victorious friend!"

Joseph excused himself from the room and Victor leaned back in his chair and closed his eyes, thinking about what Joseph had said to him. *God made me special and gives me favor to do my job for Him. That is why Joseph is always so positive! Even when things aren't so good, he knows God is there to help him.*

BUZZ . . . buzzz . . . buzzz . . . Victor awoke to the insistent wail of his alarm clock. Hitting the top to shut it off, he looked around and saw all of the familiar items in his room. There beside him on the bed was his Bible, still open to the place in Genesis where he had fallen asleep reading about his friend Joseph.

Later that day at school, Victor had trouble concentrating during history class. "It was only a dream, but it seemed so real!" he said out loud, forgetting he wasn't alone. His teacher, Coach Jacobs, frowned in Victor's direction.

"Victor, please remember this is a silent reading time," said Coach Jacobs.

"Sorry, Coach," Victor mumbled. He could hear the guys snickering behind him, but he ignored it. He tried to focus on the chapter in front of him. It would not be good to fail the quiz at the end of class.

Suddenly, Jake called out, "Coach Jacobs, I think we have a thief among us!"

"What are you talking about, Jake?" Coach Jacobs asked.

"Well, it looks like Victor here has some sticky fingers." Jake smirked as he pointed toward the floor.

Victor looked down and to his surprise saw a woman's purse sticking out of his bag.

Coach Jacobs walked over and leaned down. When he pulled out the purse, everyone started to laugh, except Coach Jacobs and Victor.

"Coach, that's not mine!"

"Well, that's comforting, Victor. You mind telling me whose it is?"

"I have no idea. I've never seen it before in my life!"

Coach Jacobs held it up and asked the class, "Does this belong to any of you?"

All of the girls shook their heads no.

"I didn't take it! I'm telling you the truth, Coach," Victor pleaded.

"Save it for Principal Tripp, Victor. I'm sure she'll want to hear what you have to say. Let's go, young man. Everyone else keep reading, I'll be right back."

On the long walk to the principal's office, all Victor could think about was what Joseph had taught him: *I am special and God loves me. He will take care of me no matter what happens.*

"Principal Tripp, we have a little problem," Coach Jacobs announced as he walked into her office and held up the purse.

Principal Tripp looked stunned. "My purse! I have been looking everywhere for that. Where did you get it?"

"I just found it in Victor's book bag. He says he doesn't know how it got there. Can you take this from here? I have to get back to my class."

Principal Tripp reached out and took the purse. "Yes, I definitely want to talk with Victor. You can return to class. Thank you."

As Coach Jacobs turned and left, Victor had never felt more alone.

Principal Tripp opened up her purse and looked inside. "Victor, where are my things?" she asked sternly. "My wallet, my keys . . . even my cell phone is gone."

"I . . . I don't know, ma'am," Victor stammered. "Really, I didn't take them. I swear!"

"Well, you must know something, Victor. You had to be involved somehow if my purse was found in your bag."

Victor didn't know what to say. He just shook his head.

"You leave me no choice, I'm afraid." Principal Tripp picked up the phone and rang her assistant. "Mrs. Ream, my purse was found but several items are missing. Would you page Officer Beckett? I think we need him to investigate the situation. Please let me know when he arrives."

She then got up from her desk and turned to Victor. "I will need you to wait in the conference room until the police officer gets here. For your sake, I hope you tell him everything."

The conference room had no windows, only a large table in the center of the room and a few metal folding chairs. Victor stared at the blank gray concrete walls.

It seemed like he had been waiting forever when the door finally opened and a police officer walked in.

"Okay, son, I'll give you one chance to tell me where the wallet, keys, and cell phone are," the officer said.

"I don't know where they are, sir. I didn't take anything. I was in history class trying to study for a quiz and the next thing I know, I am being blamed for stealing a purse because someone put it in my bag. That's the truth!" Victor pleaded, as tears of frustration welled up in his eyes.

The officer asked several more questions for which Victor had no answers. Finally, he stood up to leave and said, "Don't go anywhere, son. We're not finished with you yet."

When the door closed, Victor pulled his hoodie up and buried his head in his arms. Frustrated and scared, he began to cry. "God, where are You? You know I didn't do this. Please help me, God. Get me out of here. Help them find Principal Tripp's things. I didn't do it. God, you know I didn't do it!"

"God, you know I didn't do it!"

"Victor! Is that you?"

"What? Who is that? Where am I? It's so dark in here I can't see anything!"

"Victor, son of Jacob! It is you! I am your friend Joseph. How did you get here?"

"Joseph? Where are we? Am I dreaming again? Someone lied and said I did something terrible, but I didn't. I didn't do it. I'm innocent, but they don't believe me."

"The same thing happened to me, Victor. It was a lie that put me in this place too. But it will be okay, you will see. God is with us here and will deliver us. The truth will set us free, just wait and see. Now get some rest, we'll talk tomorrow."

"Victor, Victor . . . wake up. Victor, wake up!" Coach Jacobs shook Victor gently.

Victor startled and cried out, "But I didn't do it!"

"I know Victor, and so does Principal Tripp. The officers found her wallet, keys, and phone in Jake's locker, among other things. It seems he's been busy stealing from a lot of people lately."

Coach Jacobs put his arm around Victor's shoulders and squeezed. "You are free to go now. I called Mr. Connor, and he is on his way to pick you up."

Victor was relieved . . . and a little angry, too. "How did they figure out who had done it?"

"A couple of students overheard Jake bragging to his buddies about how he had set you up, and they reported it," answered Coach Jacobs. "I hope you understand that I had to turn in the purse and tell them you had it, Victor."

Still feeling emotional, Victor swallowed hard and nodded.

"But I'm proud of you for how you handled yourself, son."

"Thanks, Coach. I've been learning some things lately about how

God cares about me and how He has a plan for me."

"That's right, Victor. One of my favorite verses in the Bible, Romans 8:28, says, 'And we know that all things work together for good to them that love God, to them who are the called according to his purpose.' He has good things planned for you, Victor, even when it seems like bad things keep happening. Now what do you say that we go see if Mr. Connor has arrived yet?"

Victor nodded and followed Coach Jacobs out of the office. They found Mr. Connor waiting at the front entrance to the school.

"Thanks for calling, Coach," said Mr. Connor as they shook hands. "Victor must have had a rough time of it today. I'll give you a call later this week and we can talk some more then."

"Sounds good. Have a good evening, Victor."

On the drive back to Safe Haven, Victor told Mr. Connor everything that had happened that day and also about his new dream. "Joseph was accused of doing something wrong. Someone lied about him, too. I was there with him in the dark, damp prison and he told me the truth would set me free, and it did!"

"The truth did set you free today, Victor, but there is a greater truth, and that Truth is Jesus. When you became a Christian and accepted Jesus as your Lord and Savior, He set you free from death and eternal separation from Him. He will never leave you nor forsake you."

Victor had heard Mr. Connor say these words many times, but this time they took on a whole new meaning.

For the rest of the week the entire school was buzzing with the news that Jake had been arrested for theft. Victor decided not to talk about it, but he noticed that the other kids were treating him differently. On Friday, the ride home was quiet and peaceful.

"I'm home!" Victor called as the screen door slammed behind him. He found Mrs. Connor in the kitchen, preparing an early dinner. "What are we having tonight?"

"Your favorite, Victor, lasagna."

"Wow, what's the occasion? It's not my birthday."

"You'll see, Victor, it's a surprise. But please set two more places at the table. We're having company tonight and Chase and Gracie should be home soon."

"Sure, but what about the other kids?"

"They have home visits this weekend."

"Oh yeah, I forgot. If it's okay, I'd like to go outside for a while."

"That's fine," said Mrs. Connor. "Just be sure you come in when Mr. Don gets home."

Later that evening, everyone was getting ready for dinner when the doorbell rang. Victor went to see who it was.

"Coach Jacobs and Mrs. Jacobs! Is something wrong? Why are you here?"

"Victor, remember your manners, please, and invite them in," Mrs. Connor said. "They are joining us for dinner. Come on in, folks."

"Thank you. We can't wait. It smells wonderful!" Coach said as he patted Victor on the shoulder.

Dinner that evening was delicious and the conversation was fun and filled with laughter. Finally, just as everyone was finishing up, Coach Jacobs placed a small gift-wrapped box in the center of the table. "Victor, Chase, Gracie . . . Mrs. Jacobs and I brought something for the three of you."

"Wow, can I open it?" Gracie asked with excitement.

"Certainly, sweetheart, if you'd like to." Mrs. Jacobs said with a smile.

Gracie quickly tore off the wrapping paper and opened the box.

Chase reached his hand inside. "It's just a letter and three silver rings," he said, sounding a bit disappointed.

"Let me see that!" Victor took the paper from the box and began to read it aloud.

Dear Victor, Chase, and Gracie,

Long ago, before you were born, God saw you and knew you by name. He formed you in your mother's womb and He said, "I know the plans I have for you, for good and not for evil, to give you a future and a hope."

Now, it is our hope that you will spend your future with us, as our children. We have watched you grow at church and in school, and have grown more and more in love with you. Nothing in the entire world would make us happier than for you to become our children.

We believe God has brought you into our lives as a very special gift. Adopting the three of you would be the greatest blessing we have ever known.

Love,

Matthew and Sarah Jacobs

Victor finished reading and looked up, his expression full of shock and hope. "Is this true? Do you really want all of us? But you already have a family."

Mrs. Jacobs had tears in her eyes as Coach nodded his head, smiling. "Victor, our two girls are grown and starting out on their own. But they would love for the three of you to become part of our family, if it is what you want."

Chase's mouth dropped open. He was completely speechless for the first time in his life.

Gracie looked first at Victor, who nodded ever so slightly, and she then ran over and wrapped her arms around Mrs. Jacobs' neck.

"Are you serious?" Victor asked with a little hesitation. "Does this mean I can't call you Coach Jacobs anymore?"

"This kind of change always takes some time to get used to. You can just call us whatever you feel comfortable with. Coach is fine for now, and when you're ready, you can call us Mom and Dad. Nothing would make us happier."

Mr. Connor's face was beaming. "Kids, we have been praying with the Jacobs for a couple of years now, waiting for God to show them who they should adopt. God spoke to their hearts and told them you three were meant to be their children."

"The rings are all engraved with the same message, *'Adoption—Our gift to you and you to us,'*" Coach Jacobs said as he gave each child their new ring.

Chase finally spoke up, "You mean we're going to be a real family, forever and ever?"

"Forever and ever!" Mrs. Jacobs said, coming around the table and giving each of the children a big hug.

Everyone laughed and told stories until late that night. When it was finally time for bed, Victor was too excited to sleep. He just lay quietly in his bed, holding his hand up in the air as he turned his new ring around and around on his finger.

"Adopted! We are finally going to be adopted and be part of a real family," Victor whispered softly to himself, as he finally drifted off to sleep.

Victor looked around in surprise at the sound of joyful music playing. He was amazed to find himself seated at an enormous banquet table, covered from one end to the other with every kind of delicious food he could imagine.

"Victor, welcome back!" called Joseph from the head of the table. "These are four of my brothers and my father, Jacob, who have escaped the famine in Canaan. We are celebrating tonight that we are all together again!"

Victor smiled broadly and waved his hand in the air. "Look, Joseph! See my ring! I belong now. I am part of a forever family!"

"I told you so, my friend," Joseph replied. "God is always faithful!"

That was the last time Victor dreamed of Joseph. But it wasn't long before Victor, along with his brother and sister, was officially adopted by Coach and Sarah Jacobs. His new life as Victor Jacobs began, and having a real family changed everything. Victor will always remember God's love and faithfulness to him.

For you did not receive the spirit of bondage again to fear, but you received the Spirit of adoption by whom we cry out, "Abba! Father!"

—*Romans 8:15* NKJV

The Florida Baptist Children's Homes and the Leslie and Bonnie Trawick Foundation have joined together to make Victor's Dream available to all children in the Florida foster care program. When someone purchases a copy of Victor's Dream, a second book will be provided free of charge to a child in foster care. The Florida Baptist Children's Homes provides Christ-centered services to abused, neglected, and orphaned children in Florida and in the developing world through our international childcare program. We have been ministering to orphaned and disadvantaged children since 1904. The Trawick family has supported the Children's Homes' ministry for more than forty years and has generously provided the resources for this project. We are delighted to be able to put this wonderful book in the hands of thousands of foster children in Florida and beyond. We pray that the book's message of hope will inspire and encouragechildren in foster care everywhere to live in the light of Christ and His ability to transform their life into a beautiful testimony of God's grace. Learn more about foster care, adoption, and the ministry of the Florida Baptist Children's Homes at www.FBCHomes.org.

Deborah Ehler Polston resides in Florida with her husband, Justice Ricky Polston, and their six adopted sons. They also have four adult daughters, three sons-in-law, and three grandchildren. Deborah holds a mass communications degree, using her writing and speaking skills to advocate for children.

The Florida Secretary of the Department of Children and Families appointed Mrs. Polston to the Child Protection Task Force which is examining a number of issues to help improve Florida's child protection system. Deborah is also on several boards advocating for the state's children.

Florida's governor named Deborah as Florida's Point of Light Recipient for demonstrating exemplary service to the community by speaking to churches, civic groups, the media, and the Florida Legislature on behalf of foster children, also encouraging families to pursue special needs adoptions. Please visit www.deborahpolston.com.

Jay Montgomery was adopted close to birth by two of the most loving and supportive Christian parents he could ever dream possible. He's been illustrating for close to twenty years now in the Atlanta, Georgia area with a long client list of companies such as Oxford University Press, *New York Times*, *Christianity Today*, Coca-Cola, Comcast, Chick-Fil-A, ESPN, and Cartoon Network. He currently teaches illustration at Savannah College of Art & Design in Atlanta. While not working he enjoys putting smiles on the faces of his kids, Jack and Suzanne. To see more of his work please visit www.jaymontgomery.com.